It was very busy at the fair.

There were crowds of people.

Crowds of people for Mr Tickle to tickle!

Which was why Mr Tickle loved going to the Christmas Fair.

There were lots of stalls at the fair selling everything you could ever want for the perfect Christmas.

There was a tree decoration stall and a toy stall and a cake stall and a pudding stall.

There was even a stocking stall.

Little Miss Christmas' Christmas stockings.

Silly old Mr Silly!

There was ice skating on the frozen pond.

Look out Mr Bump!

Look out Little Miss Whoops!

Look out Mr Clumsy!

CRASH!

There were reindeer rides.

Mr Muddle was in his usual muddle.

Poor old Rudolph, he didn't know whether he was coming or going!

There were sleigh rides through the snowy woods.

"Jingle bells, jingle bells, jingle all the way ...
Oh what fun it is to ride in a one-horse open sleigh!"

And there was Santa's Grotto.

Father Christmas had flown in from the North Pole with a huge sack full of presents.

Mr Bounce couldn't stay still long enough to tell Father Christmas what he wanted for Christmas!

BOUNCE!

BOUNCE!

BOUNCE!

"Now, where to start?" thought Mr Tickle.

Mr Greedy was standing at a festive treats stall busily buying gingerbread men and candy canes.

Lots of gingerbread men and candy canes.

In fact, all of the gingerbread men and candy canes!

Mr Tickle reached out his extraordinarily long arm and tickled Mr Greedy.

But nothing happened.

Mr Greedy did not leap up in surprise.

He did not roll around on the ground laughing.

He did not react at all.

Mr Tickle was very puzzled.

Mr Tickle walked over to the Ferris wheel.

Mr Dizzy was going round and round getting even more dizzy than usual.

Mr Tickle reached up with one of his very long arms and tickled Mr Dizzy.

But it was just the same as when he had tried to tickle Mr Greedy.

Nothing happened!

Mr Tickle tried tickling the carol singers.

Nothing!

He tried to tickle the toffee apple seller.

Nothing!

No tickles to speak of.

A complete lack of tickles, in fact.

A tickleless day.

Poor Mr Tickle.

Whatever could be wrong?

He had lost his ticklyness!

And then Mr Tickle had a thought.

He looked all the long, long way along his extraordinarily long arms to his hands.

Hands wearing gloves.

Gloves!

"Of course!" exclaimed Mr Tickle, and with a large grin, he took off his gloves and reached out one of those extraordinarily long arms and tickled …

Now, who do you think he tickled?

I'll give you a clue.

He is very jolly.

That's right!

Father Christmas!

"Hee! Hee! Hee!" chuckled Father Christmas.

"Ha! Ha! Ha!" laughed Father Christmas.

And then finally …

"HO! HO! HO!" boomed Father Christmas.